W9-CTT-855

Flicka, Ricka, Dicka
and the
THREE KITTENS

MAJ LINDMAN

ALBERT WHITMAN & COMPANY
Morton Grove, Illinois

The Snipp, Snapp, Snurr Books
Snipp, Snapp, Snurr and the Buttered Bread
Snipp, Snapp, Snurr and the Gingerbread
Snipp, Snapp, Snurr and the Red Shoes
Snipp, Snapp, Snurr and the Reindeer
Snipp, Snapp, Snurr and the Yellow Sled
Snipp, Snapp, Snurr Learn to Swim

The Flicka, Ricka, Dicka Books
Flicka, Ricka, Dicka Bake a Cake
Flicka, Ricka, Dicka and the Big Red Hen
Flicka, Ricka, Dicka and the Little Dog
Flicka, Ricka, Dicka and the New Dotted Dresses
Flicka, Ricka, Dicka and the Three Kittens
Flicka, Ricka, Dicka and Their New Friend

Library of Congress Cataloging-in-Publication Data
Lindman, Maj.
Flicka, Ricka, Dicka and the three kittens/
written & illustrated by Maj Lindman.
p.   cm.
Summary: When their aunt and uncle's cat disappears while
they are supposed to be taking care of it, three young sisters
frantically look for it and get quite a surprise.
ISBN 0-8075-2500-6
[1. Cats—Fiction. 2. Triplets—Fiction. 3. Sweden—Fiction.]
I. Title. II. Title: Three Kittens.
PZ7.L659Fi 1994   94-13628
[E]—dc20   CIP   AC

Copyright ©1994 by Albert Whitman & Company.
Published in 1994 by Albert Whitman & Company,
6340 Oakton Street, Morton Grove, Illinois 60053.
Published simultaneously in Canada by
General Publishing, Limited, Toronto.
All rights reserved. No part of this book may be reproduced
or transmitted in any form or by any means, electronic or
mechanical, including photocopying, recording, or by any
information storage and retrieval system, without permission
in writing from the publisher.
Printed in the United States of America.
10 9 8 7 6 5 4 3

The text is set in Futura Book and Bookman Light Italic.

A Flicka, Ricka, Dicka Book

Mitzi was walking between them, purring.

Flicka, Ricka, and Dicka were three little girls who lived in Sweden. They had blue eyes and yellow hair, and they looked very much alike.

One sunny afternoon Flicka, Ricka, and Dicka went to see Uncle Jon and Aunt Helga, who lived in a little yellow house not far away. Mitzi, their big black-and-white cat, lived with them.

When the three little girls got to the little yellow house, they saw Aunt Helga, Uncle Jon, and Mitzi outside.

Aunt Helga had on her hat. A coat and pocketbook were on her arm. Uncle Jon wore his hat and overcoat. Beside him was a traveling bag.

Mitzi was walking between them, purring, just as though she knew they were going away.

As the three little girls ran up, Flicka asked, "Where are you going?"

"We must go to our daughter," Aunt Helga told them. "We must leave at once. But what can we do with Mitzi? She will be hungry, and there will be no one to give her milk or fish."

"Come, come," said Uncle Jon. "We'll be gone only a few days. Mitzi can catch mice."

"There's not a mouse about the house!" said Aunt Helga.

"Can't we give Mitzi her milk and fish?" asked Ricka as she took the cat in her arms. "We'd like to."

"Will you, dears?" said Aunt Helga, smiling. "Here's the key to the house and some money to buy milk and fish. We'd be very grateful to you."

Flicka took the key and the money.

Flicka took the key and the money.

We will take good care of Mitzi," said Dicka. "We'll buy her fresh milk and fish every day. We'll play with her, too. She won't be lonely. We'll all have fun."

"Thank you, girls," said Uncle Jon. "I feel much better about going away now!"

"It is late," said Aunt Helga. "We must catch the train. Will you girls get a pitcher from the house and buy some milk for Mitzi right away? She needs fish for supper, too."

"Of course we will," Flicka, Ricka, and Dicka answered.

Aunt Helga and Uncle Jon hurried away. The three little girls found the pitcher. Then they took it to be filled with fresh milk.

They took the pitcher to be filled with fresh milk.

Flicka paid for the milk, and Ricka carried the pitcher carefully.

They saw a woman in a striped apron selling fish. "We would like to buy a fish," said Flicka.

"Which fish do you want?" asked the woman in the striped apron.

"We don't want a big fish," said Flicka.

"But we certainly don't want a little fish," said Ricka, "for Mitzi is a big cat."

"Why not get a middle–sized, flat fish for your cat?" said the woman. "How much can you spend?"

Flicka showed her a coin, and the woman picked out a fish. Flicka paid for it, and Dicka carried it to the little yellow house.

Flicka showed her a coin.

Mitzi stood waiting for them at the door. Ricka got a saucer and filled it full of milk. She put it on the floor. Then Dicka set down the fish.

"Let us see what Mitzi eats first," said Flicka. "That will show whether she likes milk or fish better."

Mitzi sniffed the milk. Then she sat in front of the fish, wrapped her tail about her, and ate and ate until only the bones were left. Then Mitzi drank the milk.

"Did you ever see anything move faster than Mitzi's pink tongue when she drinks milk?" asked Ricka.

All that afternoon Mitzi and the three little girls played together. When Flicka, Ricka, and Dicka went home to supper, they left Mitzi asleep in the kitchen chair.

Then Mitzi drank the milk.

Early the next morning Flicka, Ricka, and Dicka hurried over to the little yellow house. When they opened the door with the big key, Mitzi came right outside, purring.

But just at that moment a brown-and-white dog ran by. Mitzi hissed. The dog barked. Then around the house ran Mitzi, the dog racing after her, barking and barking!

As the dog came close, Mitzi ran up an elm tree. Up and up she climbed, almost to the top, for she was badly frightened.

The three little girls chased the dog away. But Mitzi stayed in the tree all day long and would not come down. When the children went home for supper, Mitzi was still in the elm.

Mitzi ran up an elm tree.

Flicka, Ricka, and Dicka were so upset they forgot to close and lock the door of the little yellow house.

The three little girls could hardly sleep that night, for they were thinking about Mitzi in the tree. Was she hungry and cold?

Very early the next morning they went back to the little yellow house. They looked in the elm tree. But Mitzi was not there.

They ran around the house, calling, "Mitzi, Mitzi, pretty kitty!" But no little cat came to meet them.

They ran up and down the street calling, "Mitzi, Mitzi!" They looked in every tree for her.

Flicka asked the policeman, "Have you seen a black-and-white cat?"

The policeman shook his head. "No."

"Have you seen a black–and–white cat?"

Flicka, Ricka, and Dicka looked *everywhere* for Mitzi. They called and called.

"Oh, dear," said Dicka. "Why did we ever promise to take good care of Mitzi! Now she is lost."

"Aunt Helga and Uncle Jon will be so unhappy," said Flicka.

When they told Mother about it, she said, "Children, you must find Mitzi. You promised to take good care of her, you know."

The three little girls even climbed a roof to ask the chimney sweep if he had seen a black–and–white cat.

"I couldn't tell the color from here," he said, "but I saw a cat run down into that basement over there."

"I saw a cat run down into that basement over there."

Thank you, thank you," they said as they climbed down. "We'll look in the basement." And they ran down the basement stairs of the house across the street.

"Mitzi," called Flicka.

"Pretty kitty," called Ricka.

"Come here," called Dicka.

Ricka stopped near the basement door. In a dark corner, near a barrel, was a cat with yellow eyes.

Ricka looked at the cat carefully. Then she said slowly, "No, that's not Mitzi. That's a cat we've never seen before."

The three little girls went back up the stairs. "Where can Mitzi be?" they asked each other sadly.

In a dark corner, near a barrel, was a cat with yellow eyes.

We have looked everywhere," said Flicka. "We've called and called."

"We have looked in the trees and on the roofs," said Ricka.

"We have even asked the policeman if he has seen a black—and—white cat," said Dicka. "Whatever shall we tell Aunt Helga?"

The three little girls sat down on the doorstep of the little yellow house and began to cry.

"Poor, poor Mitzi," sobbed Ricka. "She's been lost for ever so long."

"We promised to take such good care of her," sobbed Flicka.

Then Ricka looked up.

There on the walk stood Aunt Helga and Uncle Jon.

Then Ricka looked up.

You haven't seen Mitzi for ever so long?" asked Uncle Jon. "We haven't been gone that long! If you have looked everywhere outside, then she's probably in our house."

"I never knew a cat that liked a house better!" exclaimed Aunt Helga. "There's a basket in my room where she always goes for a long nap. Probably you left the door open, and she ran in. Let's go and see."

The three little girls ran into the yellow house. They hurried to Aunt Helga's room.

And there was Mitzi! She was curled happily in a basket—with three little kittens.

One kitten was gray. One was white. And one was black–and–white.

Mitzi was curled happily in a basket—with three little kittens.

In the weeks that followed, it was Flicka who liked the gray kitten.

Dicka always played with the white kitten. And Ricka liked the black-and-white kitten best.

The three little girls and the three little kittens were always together.

"I do believe you hate to leave those kittens to go home to supper," Uncle Jon often said, laughing.

Then one day Flicka, Ricka, and Dicka had a birthday. Uncle Jon and Aunt Helga came over carrying three green baskets. In each basket was a kitten!

"Happy birthday," Uncle Jon and Aunt Helga said, and they gave each little girl the kitten she liked best.

They gave each little girl the kitten she liked best.